First published by Parragon in 2011

Parragon
Queen Street House
4 Queen Street
Bath BA1 1HE, UK

ISBN 978-1-4454-3971-6

Printed in China

"Say Please, Little Bear"

PaRragon

Bath · New York · Singapore · Hong Kong · Cologne · Delhi
Melbourne · Amsterdam · Johannesburg · Auckland · Shenzhen

Daddy Bear and Little Bear were on the way to Kindergarten.
But Little Bear kept wandering off.

"Keep hold of my hand, Little Bear!" said Daddy Bear.

"Go gently, Little Bear!" said Daddy Bear.

"Little Bear, it isn't nice to snatch!"

"It's better when
we share, Little Bear,"
said Daddy Bear.

Later, Daddy Bear took Little Bear to
Little Bunny's birthday party.
They went shopping on the way.
"Please hold my hand, Little Bear!"
said Daddy wearily.

Then something in the shop window
gave Daddy Bear an idea.
"Look, Little Bear," he said.
"That mouse wants
to speak to us!"

TOYS

"Mouse wants to come to the party too, Little Bear," said Daddy Bear. "But he hates to be late!"

They reached Little Bunny's party on time.
Mouse whispered in Daddy Bear's ear.

"Mouse says, excuse me, please."

Little Bear ran to play on the train.
Mouse whispered in Daddy Bear's ear.
"Mouse says,
can she have
a ride on the
train, please?"

Little Bear snatched the popcorn from his friends.
Mouse whispered in Daddy Bear's ear.
"Mouse says, would *you* like some popcorn, Bunny and Mole?"

When it was
time to go,
Little Bear
stood silently
on the doorstep.
"Mouse says,
thank you for
having me,"
said Daddy.

Little Bear looked at Mouse. Then he looked at Daddy Bear. Then he looked at Little Bunny's mom, and said, "And thank you for having me."

"Oh, thank you for coming,
Little Bear," smiled Little Bunny's mom.

"You and Mouse can come
and play anytime."

"Mouse likes the way
you said thank you,"
said Daddy Bear.

"And so do I."